Lisa Shost
&
Jim Paul

DUKE
BLUE DEVILS

BY BRIAN HOWELL

Printed in the United States of America,
North Mankato, Minnesota
102011
012012

 THIS BOOK CONTAINS AT LEAST 10% RECYCLED MATERIALS.

Editor: Chrös McDougall
Copy Editor: Anna Comstock
Series design and cover production: Craig Hinton
Interior production: Kelsey Oseid

Photo Credits: Ed Reinke/AP Images, cover, 1; Charles Arbogast/AP Images, 4; Mark Humphrey/AP Images, 6; Amy Sancetta/AP Images, 9, 43 (bottom left); David Longstreath/AP Images, 10, 28, 42 (bottom right); Jae C. Hong/AP Images, 12; Diana Pappas/Alamy, 15; AP Images, 16, 22, 24, 27, 42 (bottom left), 43 (top); Kevin C. Cox/Getty Images, 19, 42 (top); Jake Drake/Cal Sports Media/AP Images, 20; Ron Heflin/AP Images, 31; Bob Jordan/AP Images, 32; Brian Gadbery/NCAA Photos/AP Images, 34; Dave Martin/AP Images, 37; Gerry Broome/AP Images, 38; Chris Steppig/NCAA Photos/AP Images, 41, 43 (bottom right); Frank Tozier/Alamy, 44

Design elements: Matthew Brown/iStockphoto

Library of Congress Cataloging-in-Publication Data
Howell, Brian, 1974-
  Duke Blue Devils / by Brian Howell.
    p. cm. -- (Inside college basketball)
  Includes index.
  ISBN 978-1-61783-281-9
  1. Duke Blue Devils (Basketball team)--History--Juvenile literature. 2. Duke University--Basketball--History--Juvenile literature. I. Title.
  GV885.43.D85H68 2012
  796.323'6309756563--dc23
                          2011038228

TABLE OF CONTENTS

Christian Laettner puts up the game-winning shot against Kentucky during the 1992 NCAA Tournament.

BLUE DEVILS REACH THE PEAK

THE DREAM OF A SECOND NATIONAL CHAMPIONSHIP IN A ROW WAS IN TROUBLE. ONLY 2.1 SECONDS REMAINED IN OVERTIME OF THE NATIONAL COLLEGIATE ATHLETIC ASSOCIATION (NCAA) TOURNAMENT QUARTERFINALS. THE DUKE UNIVERSITY MEN'S BASKETBALL TEAM—NICKNAMED THE BLUE DEVILS— TRAILED THE KENTUCKY WILDCATS BY ONE POINT. WHAT FOLLOWED IN THOSE 2.1 SECONDS WOULD GO DOWN AS ONE OF THE MOST FAMOUS MOMENTS IN COLLEGE BASKETBALL HISTORY.

It was March 28, 1992. Duke and Kentucky were locked in a battle at the Spectrum in Philadelphia, Pennsylvania. The winner would go to the Final Four and have a chance to play for a national championship. The NCAA Tournament is always one of the most exciting sporting events of the year. With Duke and Kentucky playing each other, this game was particularly special.

As men's basketball programs, Duke and Kentucky both had long histories of success. Both schools had especially

good teams during the 1992 season. Kentucky's Wildcats were ranked number six in the nation. They had won 29 of their 35 games before meeting Duke in the tournament. But as good as the Wildcats were, Duke was favored coming into their NCAA Tournament game. The Blue Devils had won the championship in 1991. And they were even better in 1992, losing just two games total that season. They came into the tournament ranked number one in the country.

Part of what makes the NCAA Tournament so popular, however, is the unexpected. Underdogs frequently upset the favorites in the tournament. That is why it is nicknamed March Madness. And on this night, Kentucky did its best to upset the defending champions.

After 40 minutes of regulation, the game was tied. So the teams went into overtime. With 2.1 seconds left in the five-minute overtime period, Kentucky took a 103–102 lead. Duke would need a miracle to stay alive in its quest for another national championship.

In search of that miracle, Duke turned to its two superstars. Forward Grant Hill and center Christian Laettner are considered two of the best players in Duke history. In fact, many consider them to be two of the best players in college basketball history. And with 2.1 seconds to play and a season hanging in the balance, Hill and Laettner teamed up for a miracle.

Hill's job was to get the ball in bounds from behind Kentucky's basket. That was not an easy job. With only 2.1 seconds to play, Hill would have

LAETTNER SHINES

Center Christian Laettner enjoyed one of the greatest college basketball careers ever. The New York native led Duke to the Final Four in all four of his years there. As a senior in 1992, he was the National and Atlantic Coast Conference (ACC) Player of the Year. After the 1992 title, he was the only college player on the "Dream Team," which won a gold medal for the United States at the Olympic Games. Laettner then played 13 seasons in the National Basketball Association (NBA). Duke retired his No. 32 jersey. And Laettner was named to the College Basketball Hall of Fame.

However, it was his performance against Kentucky in that 1992 Tournament game that defined his career—he made all 20 of the shots he attempted in the game (10 free throws, 10 field goals), including the game-winner at the buzzer.

to throw the ball approximately 78 feet across the 94-foot court. Then Laettner, the 1992 NCAA Player of the Year, would have to catch it and immediately shoot. Although Hill did not have any Kentucky players guarding him, it was still a tough play. He had tried the same pass a couple weeks earlier in a game, and it had not worked.

Still, Duke coach Mike Krzyzewski decided to give the play another chance. The Blue Devils were confident it would work. "I told [Hill] if we ever had another chance to run it again and he threw it straight, we'd win," Laettner said.

The crowd rose to its feet as Hill threw the ball down court. It went right to Laettner, who caught it with his back to the basket and two Wildcats defenders guarding him. Laettner dribbled the ball once and then turned and shot the ball over the defenders. As the ball slipped through the basket, Duke players, coaches, and fans celebrated. The 104–103 win sent Duke to another Final Four.

"Throughout the game, we were aware we were watching something special," said Verne Lundquist, who broadcast the game on television. "And when Laettner made that shot, Lenny Elmore, my broadcast partner, [and I] took our headsets off and neither one of us

SAY THAT AGAIN?

Trying to spell, or say, Duke coach Mike Krzyzewski's name has troubled many people. That's why the legendary Duke coach is generally referred to as "Coach K." His last name is pronounced "sha-SHEF-skee."

Center Christian Laettner celebrates his game-winning shot against Kentucky in the 1992 NCAA Tournament.

were saying much, just kind of deeply exhaling, because we knew that we'd just seen maybe the best game ever."

Many agreed with Lundquist. After all, the game featured two iconic basketball programs. It also featured a remarkable finish. The lead changed hands five times in the last 31.5 seconds. The last of those lead

changes came when Laettner sank his thrilling shot. Years later, the finish is still played over and over during the NCAA Tournament.

"I told the kids in the locker room, 'I think we've just been a part of history,'" Krzyzewski said after the game. "I really am stunned. Did that really just happen?"

The Duke players had little time to celebrate. They were soon on their way to Minneapolis, Minnesota, for the Final Four. There, they defeated the Indiana Hoosiers and then the Michigan Wolverines to claim their second straight national championship. But it was the Blue Devils' dramatic win over Kentucky that fans remembered most. It was the defining moment for what some consider the best college basketball team in history.

Laettner was the biggest star of that group. A three-time All-American, he led the Blue Devils to the national championship game in 1990, 1991, and 1992. Hill and point guard Bobby Hurley also were stars during that remarkable run for the Blue Devils. It was Hurley, in fact, who earned NCAA Tournament Most Valuable Player (MVP) honors in 1992.

Since the early 1900s, when Duke was known as Trinity College, basketball has played a major role in the school's history. Just three teams—Kentucky, North Carolina, and Kansas—have won more games through 2011. Only four teams—University of California, Los Angeles (UCLA); Kentucky; Indiana; and North Carolina—have won more than Duke's four championships. But of all the great Duke teams, many consider that 1992 squad to be the best.

"We're pretty secure in our place in history," Hill said, "and we feel we're up there with those UCLA teams."

KING OF THE HILL

Grant Hill was one of the youngest players on Duke's 1991 and 1992 title teams, but he also was one of the best. Hill, whose father Calvin Hill played in the National Football League, led Duke to three Final Fours and two national titles from 1991 to 1994. In 1993, Hill was named the best defensive player in the country. In 1994, he was named the ACC Player of the Year. And in 2010–11, Hill played his 16th NBA season. Hill's jersey, No. 33, is retired at Duke.

Duke's mascot has been the Blue Devil since 1929. It debuted at a Duke football game.

2

GAINING NATIONAL ATTENTION

TRINITY COLLEGE OPENED IN DURHAM, NORTH CAROLINA, DURING THE 1800s. TIES TO THE METHODIST CHURCH KEPT TRINITY ALIVE THROUGH THE CIVIL WAR, RECONSTRUCTION, AND WORLD WAR I. THEN IN 1924, TRINITY MOVED TO A NEW CAMPUS AND WENT THROUGH OTHER CHANGES AS WELL. BECAUSE OF THAT, IT ALSO GOT A NEW NAME—DUKE UNIVERSITY. IT WAS NAMED FOR THE DUKE FAMILY, WHICH PROVIDED FINANCIAL AND OTHER SUPPORT TO THE SCHOOL FOR YEARS.

Even before the school took on the Duke name, basketball was a popular game there. Wilbur Wade "Cap" Card was an exceptional baseball player at Trinity. He is best known, however, for introducing college basketball to the state of North Carolina. After graduating from Trinity, Card later became the school's athletic director. In 1906, he organized the first college basketball game in the state where basketball now is king. Coached by Card, Trinity played neighboring Wake Forest on March 2, 1906. Wake Forest

DUKE'S FIRST ALL-AMERICAN

Through 2011, more than 30 Duke players have been named All-Americans. The first was Bill Werber, who earned All-America honors in 1930. An exceptional guard during his time, Werber helped Duke go 39–15 during his three years on the basketball team. He was actually a better baseball player, though. Werber helped Duke's baseball team go 43–17–1 from 1928 to 1930. After college, he played 11 seasons of Major League Baseball, even winning a World Series with the Cincinnati Reds in 1940. Werber died in 2009 at the age of 100.

won the game 24–10, but Trinity's love of the sport was only beginning.

Trinity/Duke spent the next 20-plus years establishing its basketball program. Card coached the team for seven seasons. Then from 1912 to 1928, the team had 10 different coaches. There was no national championship tournament at the time, but Trinity/Duke had some great seasons. Their best finish during that period was 20–4 in 1916–17.

Duke basketball took a giant leap forward in 1928–29. That year, the school hired assistant football coach Eddie Cameron to coach the basketball team. The school also joined the Southern Conference. Duke's men's basketball team instantly became one of its best teams. In fact, Duke surprised many by reaching the conference championship game in each of Cameron's first two seasons.

In 14 seasons as Duke's coach, Cameron turned the Blue Devils into one of the nation's best teams. Cameron won 226 games and produced wins in 69.5 percent of the games he coached. The Blue Devils reached the conference championship game eight times in his 14 seasons, winning

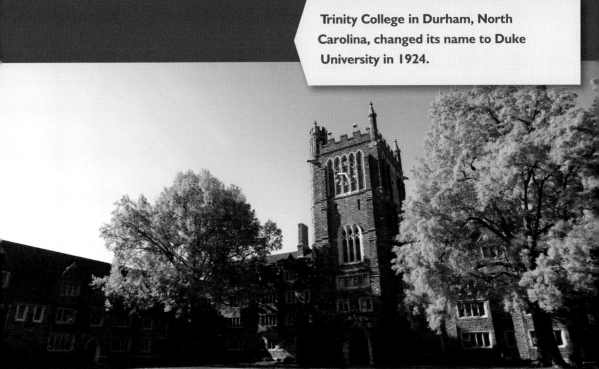

it three times. Cameron's last Duke team, in 1941–42, had a sensational 22–2 record, including 15–1 in conference games.

Shortly after the 1942 season, however, Duke athletic director and football coach Wallace Wade was called to duty for the US Army in World War II. Cameron took over Wade's duties. But in December of that year, Cameron decided being athletic director, football coach, and basketball coach was too stressful. He resigned from his duties as basketball coach. Assistant coach Gerry Gerard took over.

The Blue Devils have enjoyed dozens of great seasons since Cameron left. But Cameron got the train rolling. That is why, in 1972, Duke University named its basketball arena after the legendary coach— Cameron Indoor Stadium.

GAINING NATIONAL ATTENTION

Guard Dick Groat was an All-American for Duke in 1951 and 1952.

3

SUCCESS CONTINUES

COACH EDDIE CAMERON HELPED DUKE BECOME A TOP COLLEGE BASKETBALL TEAM BEFORE RESIGNING FROM HIS POSITION AFTER THE 1941–42 SEASON. THE BLUE DEVILS CONTINUED TO BE ONE OF THE BEST TEAMS IN THE SOUTHERN CONFERENCE AFTER HE LEFT, THANKS TO GERRY GERARD AND HAROLD BRADLEY.

Gerard took over as head coach before the 1942–43 season. He guided the Blue Devils to a 20–6 record and into the Southern Conference championship game. The Blue Devils were considered strong favorites to win that game, but they lost 56–40 to George Washington University.

Despite the loss to George Washington, Gerard kept the winning tradition alive during his eight seasons in charge. He coached 209 games and won 131 of them. In six of Gerard's eight seasons, the Blue Devils played in the Southern Conference championship game, winning two.

GROAT LEADS DUKE

Today, Dick Groat is most remembered as a baseball player. Before playing 14 seasons in the majors, Groat was a two-sport star at Duke. He was an All-American in baseball, helping Duke reach the College World Series for the first time. And in basketball, Groat was one of the greatest Blue Devils of all time.

Groat was the Southern Conference Athlete of the Year in 1951 and 1952. He also was the National Player of the Year in basketball in 1952. As a junior in 1951, he set a national record with 831 points for the season. Shortly after playing his last basketball game with the Blue Devils, Groat became the first player in Duke history to have his jersey—No. 10—retired. Groat is a member of the National Collegiate Basketball Hall of Fame and the Collegiate Baseball Hall of Fame.

Poor health led to Gerard leaving the Blue Devils after the 1949–50 season. He was very ill in 1949, but recovered to coach one last season. In November 1950, however, his health left him no choice but to retire.

Gerard, who also organized and coached Duke's soccer team for 11 years, died of cancer about two months after his retirement. He was only 47 years old.

"Coach Gerard lived and worked in the highest tradition of good sportsmanship, and his quiet courage and innate goodness won the respect of those who knew him," Duke president Hollis Edens said.

Gerard was involved in several sports in North Carolina, both as a coach and an official. Like Cameron, he enjoyed great success with the Blue Devils basketball team. And, again like Cameron, he left the team in great hands.

Duke's student fans are known as the "Cameron Crazies." Approximately 1,200 Cameron Crazies attend each home game.

Bradley took over after Gerard's retirement. He continued Duke's winning tradition during his nine seasons. In 1951 and 1952, Bradley led Duke to the Southern Conference championship game. That gave Duke 11 championship game appearances in 13 seasons.

Bradley's time as coach saw the Blue Devils gain another measure of national respect. During the 1951–52 season, the Blue Devils made their first-ever appearance in the national rankings. They finished the season ranked 12th in the Associated Press poll.

SUCCESS CONTINUES

Bradley also led Duke to its first-ever NCAA Tournament. The tournament began in 1939, but it only included eight teams until expanding to 16 in 1951. After a 20–8 regular-season record in 1954–55, Duke lost to Villanova in the first round of the tournament. As the tournament expanded, the Blue Devils soon became a regular presence there.

In addition to guiding Duke into the national rankings and into the NCAA Tournament, Bradley also guided the Blue Devils into a new conference. Duke had spent 25 seasons in the Southern Conference, which had grown to 17 members by the end of the 1953 season. After

TRIPLETS

Throughout its history, Duke has had many great players. Through 2011, however, only six have made the All-Conference first team three times. The first was Corren Youmans, who played for Gerry Gerard from 1946 to 1950. He led Duke in points in each of his three varsity seasons. Youmans also was a star receiver on the Duke football team.

that season, seven schools—Duke, Clemson, Maryland, North Carolina, North Carolina State, South Carolina, and Wake Forest—left the Southern Conference. That group of schools got together and created a new conference: the ACC. Later that year, Virginia was added to the ACC. The initial breakaway began a long association between Duke and the ACC, which was still going strong in 2011.

Duke left the Southern Conference with a sterling record. During its 25 seasons in the conference, Duke played in the tournament championship game 16 times, winning five. The Blue Devils quickly set a winning tone in the ACC too. Bradley coached the team during its first six ACC seasons. Duke won the conference title in two of those years and never finished lower than third during that time.

Like Cameron's and Gerard's, Bradley's time as Duke coach was viewed as a success. He led the Blue Devils to 165 wins in 243 games. And Duke never had a losing record during his nine seasons. Bradley left Duke after the 1959 season to become the head coach at Texas. As usual, though, Duke replaced him with another good coach—and the winning continued.

SUCCESS CONTINUES

Duke's Jay Buckley drives between two UCLA players during the 1964 NCAA Tournament championship game.

4

JOINING THE ELITE

IN 1964, NOBODY IN COLLEGE BASKETBALL COULD STOP THE UCLA BRUINS. DUKE WAS NO EXCEPTION. ALTHOUGH MANY PEOPLE THOUGHT THE BLUE DEVILS WOULD BE NATIONAL CHAMPIONS IN 1964, THEY CAME UP JUST SHORT. IN THE CHAMPIONSHIP GAME, UCLA ROLLED TO A 98–83 WIN. THE BRUINS FINISHED A PERFECT 30–0 THAT SEASON.

For Duke, it was the second disappointing finish in two years. Coached by Vic Bubas, those Duke teams featured some of the greatest players in the country. Art Heyman was a three-time All-American from 1961 to 1963. He was a great scorer and rebounder. From 1961 to 1964, Jeff Mullins was one of the best Blue Devils ever. He was a two-time All-American, in 1963 and 1964.

Led by Heyman and Mullins, the Blue Devils got to the 1963 Final Four. It was the team's first Final Four appearance. However, Duke lost in the semifinals and finished third in the country.

Duke coach Vic Bubas still held the ACC record for career winning percentage (.761) in 2011.

Heyman graduated before the 1964 season. But Mullins still shined. In fact, he led the Blue Devils to the championship game. However, the loss to UCLA meant Duke finished second.

Accepting defeat was not easy. Yet, rather than worry about the loss, Bubas looked ahead. "Last year we came back number three. This year it was number two. That leaves just one thing for next year," said Bubas, who had become Duke's coach in 1959.

Bubas was pointing toward a championship. Duke did not win the next year. But Bubas made it clear: Duke was now a championship-minded program.

Prior to Bubas taking over as coach, Duke had produced 30 seasons of winning basketball. But the Blue Devils had been to the NCAA Tournament just one time. And that trip had ended in a first-round loss.

In 1960, Bubas's first season, the Blue Devils advanced to the NCAA Tournament quarterfinals. Duke missed the tournament in 1961 and 1962. But from 1963 to 1966, Duke made the Final Four three times in four seasons.

Bubas never did win the national title he sought. But he never had a losing season either. In fact, the Blue Devils won four regular-season conference titles during his 10 seasons as coach. They won at least 20

LEGENDARY DEVILS

Two players helped Duke become a great team during the early 1960s. Forward Art Heyman was the National and ACC Player of the Year in 1963. A three-time All-American, Heyman was one of the best scorers and rebounders in school history. His career scoring average of 25.1 points per game still ranked as the best in Duke history in 2011. Forward Jeff Mullins was a two-time All-American and the ACC Player of the Year in 1964. He averaged 21.9 points per game in his career, which ranked fourth in Duke history through 2011. Duke has retired both Heyman's No. 25 and Mullins's No. 44 jerseys. After leaving Duke, Heyman was the number-one draft choice in the 1963 NBA Draft. Mullins was a three-time NBA All-Star.

games in seven of those seasons. The Blue Devils finished in the top 10 of the national rankings in each of those seven seasons.

Bubas resigned after the 1969 season. At that point, the Blue Devils had played 41 seasons of basketball since Eddie Cameron had arrived in 1928. Only one of those 41 was a losing season—way back in 1939.

Rough times were ahead, however. Bucky Waters, a former Duke assistant, replaced Bubas. He led the Blue Devils to back-to-back appearances in the National Invitation Tournament (NIT) in 1970 and 1971. Since the NCAA Tournament was relatively small at that time—with only 22 to 25 teams—the NIT was considered the *other* major tournament. Today, however, the NIT is considered the second-tier postseason tournament. All-American center Randy Denton was the star of those 1970 and 1971 teams.

Then, from 1972 to 1977, Duke struggled. Three coaches—Waters, Neill McGeachy, and Bill Foster—led Duke during those six seasons. But Duke never finished higher than fourth in the ACC standings in any of them. The Blue Devils also lost more than they won in those years, going 76–82 overall.

GMINSKI LEADS THE WAY

From 1977 to 1980, center Mike Gminski had one of the best careers of any Blue Devil in history. A three-time All-American, he was the ACC Player of the Year as a junior in 1979. Through 2011, Gminski still ranked among Duke's career leaders in scoring (fourth), rebounds (second), and blocked shots (second). Duke has retired his No. 43 jersey.

Duke's Jim Spanarkel, *right,* passes to Mike Gminski, *left,* in the 1978 Elite Eight game against Villanova.

Foster stuck with the team and eventually found success. In 1978, he became the first Duke coach to be named National Coach of the Year. That season, he guided the Blue Devils back to the national championship game. But again, they lost, this time to Kentucky. Duke could not stop Jack Givens, who scored 41 points in the 94–88 win. "It seems like he hit from every conceivable spot," Foster said.

Although they lost, the Blue Devils were back on the national stage. Center Mike Gminski, guard Jim Spanarkel, and forward Gene Banks, all three All-Americans, guided Duke back to elite status. In 1979, the Blue Devils shared the ACC regular-season title and got to the second round of the NCAA Tournament. In 1980, they got back to the Elite Eight. Foster, however, left Duke after that season to become South Carolina's coach.

JOINING THE ELITE

[27]

Coach Mike Krzyzewski helped turn Duke from a good program into one of the country's most successful programs.

5

COACH K COMES TO DUKE

FOLLOWING THE 1980 SEASON, COACH BILL FOSTER LEFT DUKE FOR SOUTH CAROLINA. LOOKING FOR A FRESH START, DUKE TURNED TO A YOUNG COACH FROM ARMY. THE SCHOOL HIRED MIKE KRZYZEWSKI IN MARCH 1980. HE WAS JUST 33 YEARS OLD.

"The boy, the young man, has established a good track record," Duke athletic director Tom Butters said upon hiring Krzyzewski.

Krzyzewski—known simply as "Coach K"—had played at Army before coaching there. In five seasons as Army's head coach, he led his team to a 73–59 overall record. He also took Army to the NIT in 1978.

When he arrived at Duke, Krzyzewski's goals were modest. "I think Duke basketball is excellent, has been excellent, and I hope to continue that tradition," he said.

Krzyzewski not only continued the tradition, but he made it better. Through the 2010–11 season—his 31st at Duke—

JOHNNY DAWKINS

When coach Mike Krzyzewski rebuilt the Duke program into a winner, he leaned heavily on point guard Johnny Dawkins. The Washington DC native was a sensation as a freshman in 1983. However, Duke finished with a losing record. But Dawkins's remarkable play helped Duke become a winner. In 1986, Dawkins was the National Player of the Year. He guided the Blue Devils to the national championship game. Dawkins left Duke as the team's all-time leading scorer, with 2,556 points. As of 2011, Dawkins ranked second, behind J. J. Redick.

Krzyzewski had guided the Blue Devils to 827 wins, 27 NCAA Tournament appearances, and four national championships. Including his wins at Army, Krzyzewski had 900 career victories as of 2011. Only Bob Knight, who had once coached Krzyzewski, had more wins in Division I men's basketball. Knight had 902.

But Krzyzewski did not get off to a great start at Duke. The Blue Devils went 17–13 and advanced to the NIT in his first season. However, he produced losing records in his second and third years.

Duke's 1983 team finished 12–17, but did so while starting four freshmen players. Toward the end of that season, Krzyzewski said the Blue Devils knew brighter days were ahead. "We've shown that there are no quitters in this program," he said. "They still have the confidence that they're going to be a fine basketball team."

The 1982–83 season was the last in which Krzyzewski coached a losing team. Beginning in 1984, the Blue Devils qualified for the NCAA Tournament 11 straight years. The streak ended in 1994–95, when Krzyzewski missed the final 19 games for health reasons. The Blue

Point guard Johnny Dawkins was the 1986 National Player of the Year.

Devils went just 4–15 in his absence. Still, Duke got back in the NCAA Tournament the next year. The 2011 season was the Blue Devils' 16th consecutive season there.

Krzyzewski's first run at the NCAA championship game came in 1986. Behind point guard Johnny Dawkins and forward Mark Alarie, the

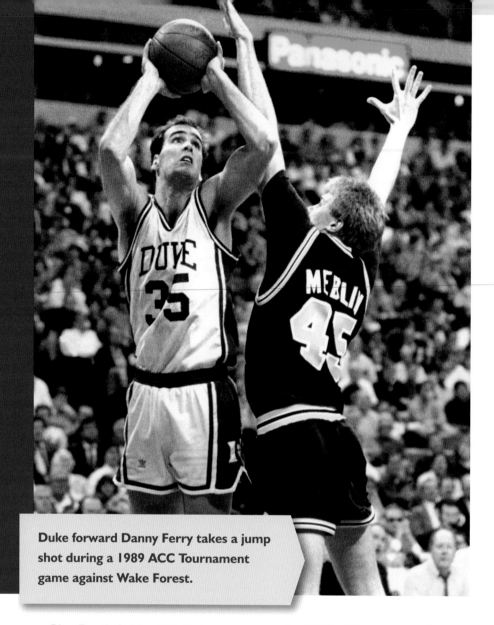

Duke forward Danny Ferry takes a jump shot during a 1989 ACC Tournament game against Wake Forest.

Blue Devils finished 37–3 that season. In the NCAA Tournament, they advanced all the way to the championship game. But once there, Duke lost to Louisville to finish second in the nation.

Two years later, Duke began a remarkable run of success that few teams in history have ever matched. The Blue Devils played in the

Final Four six times in seven years from 1988 to 1994. They played in the championship game four times and won national titles in 1991 and 1992.

Those Duke teams produced several of the best players college basketball has ever seen. Forward Danny Ferry was named the National Player of the Year in 1989. Forward Christian Laettner then earned that honor in 1992. Ferry was a two-time All-American, while Laettner earned the honor three times. Also during those years, point guard Bobby Hurley was a two-time All-American and forward Grant Hill was a three-time All-American.

Under Krzyzewski, Duke had become a bona fide elite program. And the national championships of 1991 and 1992 were only the beginning.

A LEADER OF MEN

Mike Krzyzewski's success goes beyond his wins at Duke. He led the US men's national team to a gold medal at the 2008 Olympic Games in Beijing, China. He was also an assistant coach for the US team at the 1984 and 1992 Games. In addition, Coach K has transferred his knowledge to a new generation of coaches. Several of his Duke players have gone on to become head coaches, including Tommy Amaker, Jeff Capel, Johnny Dawkins, and Quin Snyder.

"[Coach K] is everything I thought he would be and more," said NBA star Kobe Bryant, who played for Krzyzewski on the US national team. "Playing for him now, you realize why he is such a great coach. He communicates extremely well with his players. He's very intense and has a passion for what he does, and he has a great sense of humor." Krzyzewski was named to the Naismith Basketball Hall of Fame in 2001.

Forward Shane Battier dunks the ball over the Arizona Wildcats in the 2001 NCAA Tournament championship game.

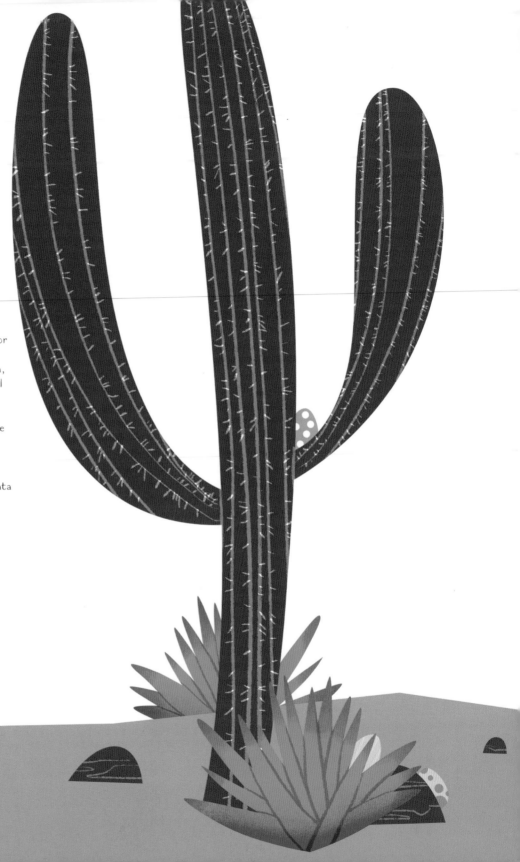

FOR NATE AND HIS
LOVE FOR BOOKS.
—J. H.

Published by Familius LLC, www.familius.com

Familius books are available at special discounts for
bulk purchases, whether for sales promotions or
for family or corporate use. For more information,
contact Familius Sales at 559-876-2170 or email
orders@familius.com.

Library of Congress Cataloging-in-Publication Data
2016952937
Print ISBN 9781942934912
eISBN 9781945547034

Printed in China

Illustrated by Jeff Harvey
Edited by Lindsay Sandberg
Cover and book design by David Miles

10 9 8 7 6 5 4 3 2 1

First Edition

A VERY BUNNY ARIZONA

A GRAND CANYON STATE EASTER ADVENTURE

BY JEFF HARVEY

You know about the eggs the Easter Bunny hides,
hard boiled and dyed or with candy inside.
Well, the next day he's back, hip-hopping around,
to gather the eggs that nobody found.

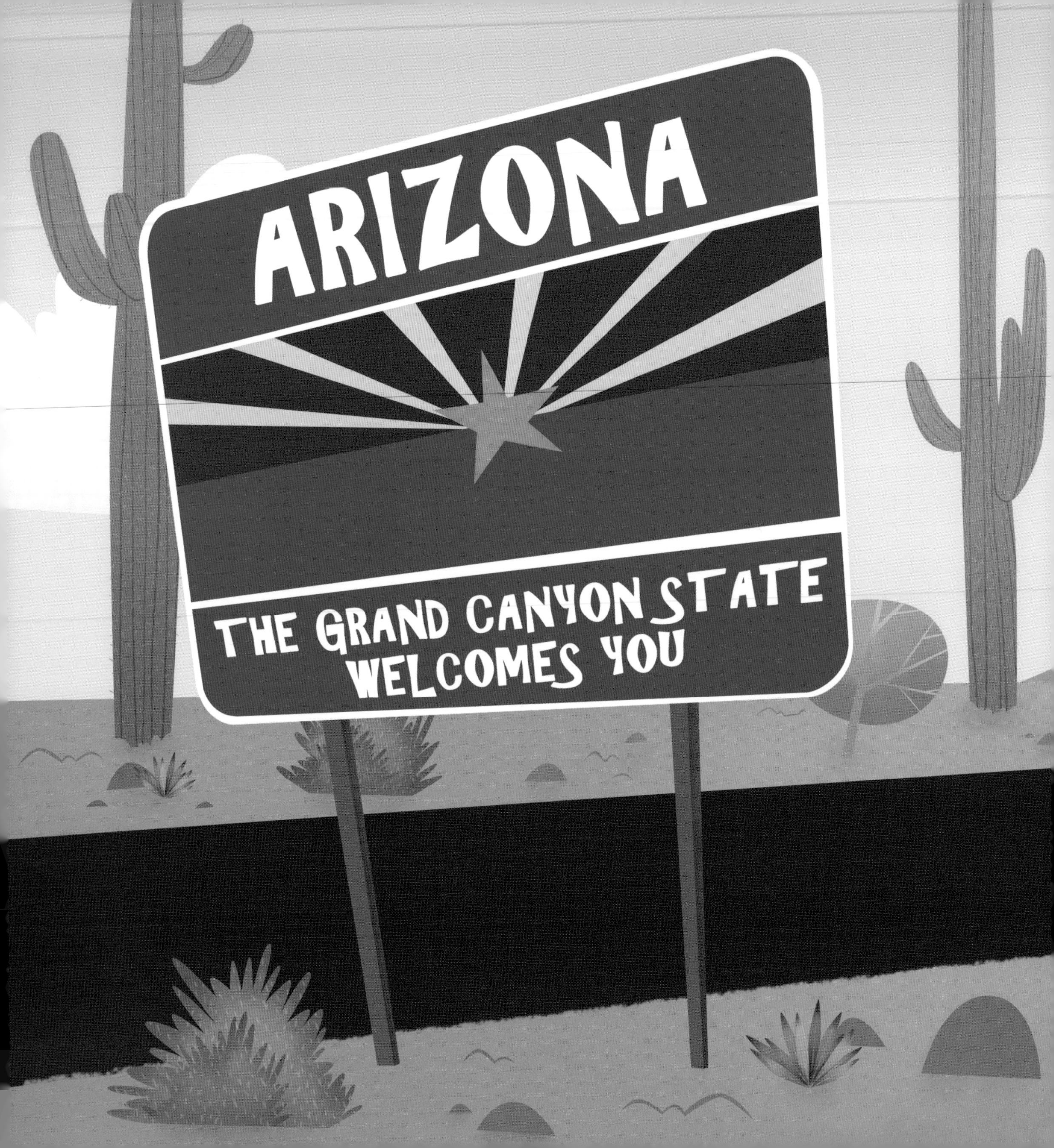
ARIZONA
THE GRAND CANYON STATE
WELCOMES YOU

So he's off to Arizona with one thing on his mind—
how many Easter eggs can you help him find?

Monument Valley is our journey's start,
so find the first egg before we depart.

The Grand Canyon is truly a beautiful sight!
Can you spot the egg from this dizzying height?

To see the whole canyon all in one day,
look for the egg on Grand Canyon Railway.

The Hoover Dam is over 700 feet tall!
But don't forget the egg; we must find them all.

The cliffs of Sedona are orange and red.
Keep an eye out — there are more eggs ahead.

Nearby at Slide Rock, there's the next egg to get.
And come with your bathing suit in case you get wet!

Step into Old Town Scottsdale, a taste of the West.
Once we spot this next egg, we're off for the rest!

Tovrea Castle is a landmark you'll love.
Find the egg down below with a view from above.

Pima Air & Space Museum
has all things sky and space.
Two eggs left to find now,
so let's pick up the pace!

Tucson Botanical Gardens grows colorful plants.
Is there an egg hiding here? Let's take a glance.

The last hidden egg is in Saguaro National Park.
Be sure to find it here before it gets dark.

Thanks for all your help today.
You really were quite great.
But I must be on my way —
I'm off to another state!